W9-CBA-261

Mark and the Molecule Maker

A portion of proceeds from the sale of Mark and the Molecule Maker will be donated to First Book, a nonprofit organization that provides new books for children in need. Learn more about their work at www.firstbook.org

Mark and the Molecule Maker

ISBN 978-0-9829506-1-6
Library of Congress Control Number: 2012946594

Printed in China by Kings Time Printing Press, Ltd.
The display type is set in Ozymandias.
Cover type is set in Gilligan's Island.

Visit our website at
www.octopusinkpress.com

Mark and the Molecule Maker

Written by Scott Sussman
Illustrated by Yves Margarita

Meet Mark.

His father is an inventor.

He and Mark's mom were sleeping while Mark lay wide-awake, tossing and turning in bed. He got up, paced back and forth, and then went downstairs for a glass of water.

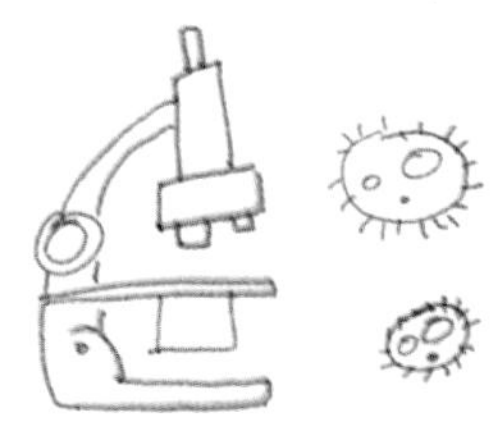

He had opened the refrigerator and was reaching for the water bottle when suddenly he heard a crash. It had come from his father's laboratory. He shut the refrigerator and then hurried down the hall.

Rockola

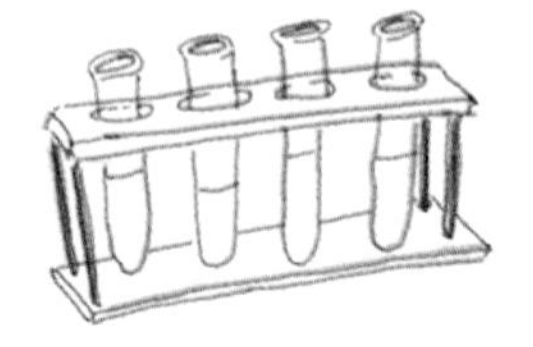

Mark put his ear against the laboratory door. He heard humming sounds, buzzes and an occasional crack. Though he knew it was against his father's rules, he turned the knob, opened the door and, for the first time ever, entered the lab alone.

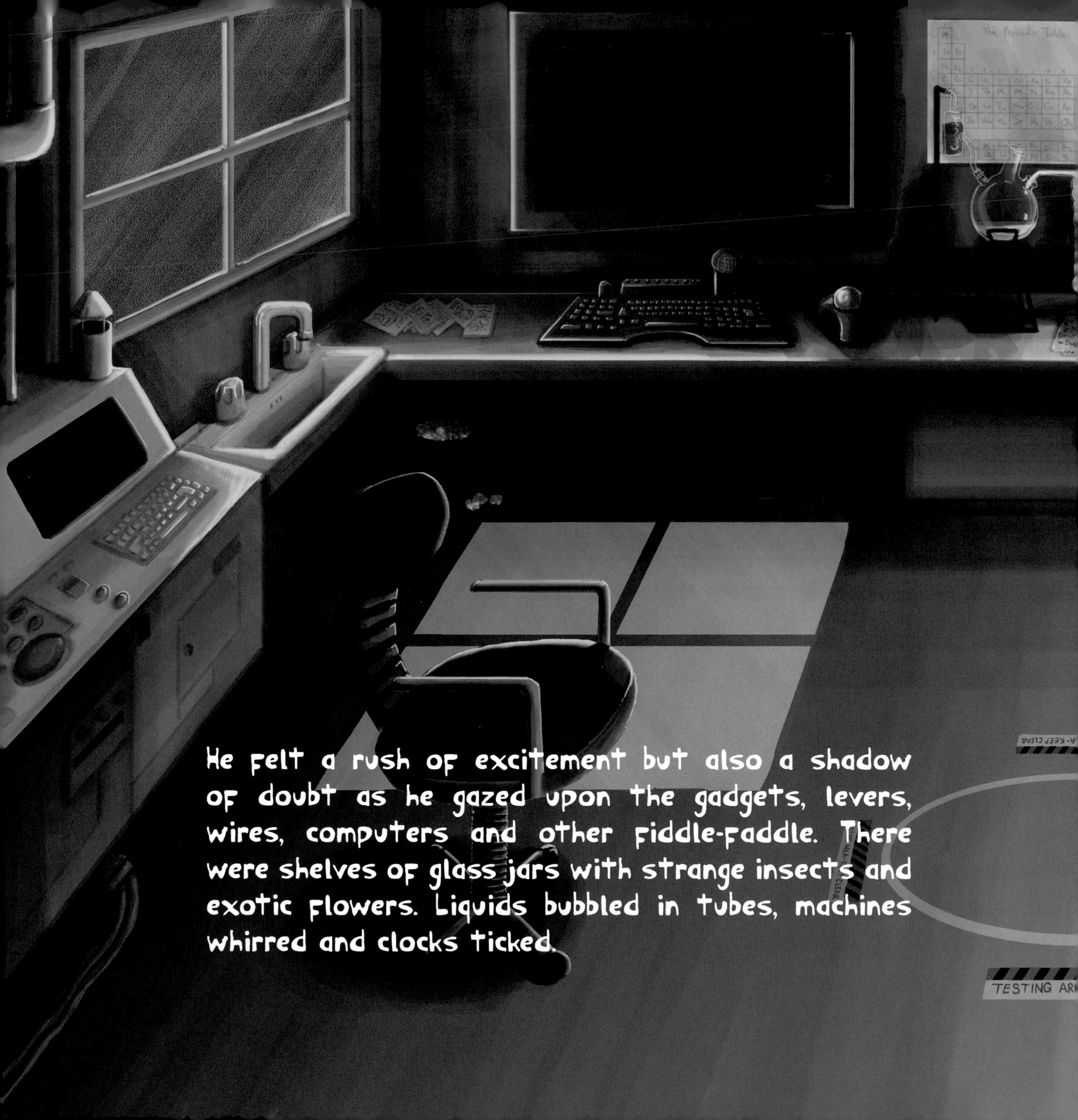

He felt a rush of excitement but also a shadow of doubt as he gazed upon the gadgets, levers, wires, computers and other fiddle-faddle. There were shelves of glass jars with strange insects and exotic flowers. Liquids bubbled in tubes, machines whirred and clocks ticked.

TESTING AREA-KEEP CLEAR

There was a remote control on top of the table. He had never seen it before. It was labeled, Molecule Maker. It had various buttons, each a different color, and one red switch on the side.

Mark picked up the Molecule Maker. He pressed the purple button. The Molecule Maker started rattling as it became hot in his hand. Then a ray of light shot out and suddenly he was face to face with a fantastic creature. It was as big as an elephant, and had a horn on its head, sparkling silver fur, and one glowing blue eye.

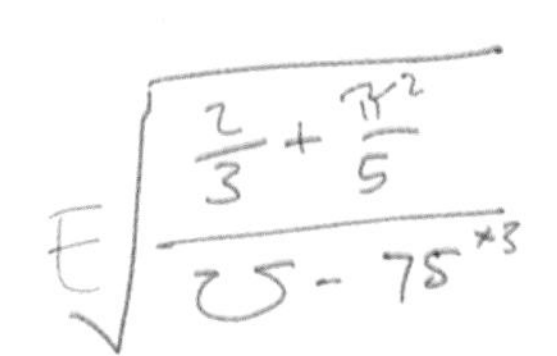

SMASH

Just like that, it leaped through the window, smashing the glass, and then hopped over the fence and dashed into the street.

Oh boy! Now I've done it! Mark thought as he stuffed the Molecule Maker into his pocket and ran after the creature, following the trail of toppled trees, crushed cars, and an overturned fire hydrant. A jet of water streamed into the air.

The creature was quick. So Mark grabbed the Molecule Maker, pushed the yellow button, and made another creature. It looked like a dinosaur with huge, white wings. He climbed up its tail, crawled across its back, and sat straddling its neck.

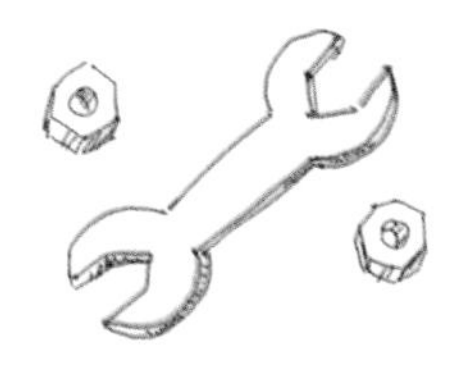

The creature galloped down the street while spreading its wings to fly. It hopped once, twice, and then Mark's heart hammered with exhilaration as they lifted off the ground and soared into the sky.

In the light of the full moon Mark found the blue-eyed creature climbing a tree in the park. It was breaking off branches, cramming them into its mouth, and chomping them like carrots.

Mark fired the Molecule Maker. The blast created a third creature as tall as a skyscraper. *Oops!*

The giant creature lifted its leg and was about to squash Mark under its monstrous foot. But Mark had an idea.

He flipped the switch on the side of the Molecule Maker, aimed and *ZAP!* The creature disappeared.

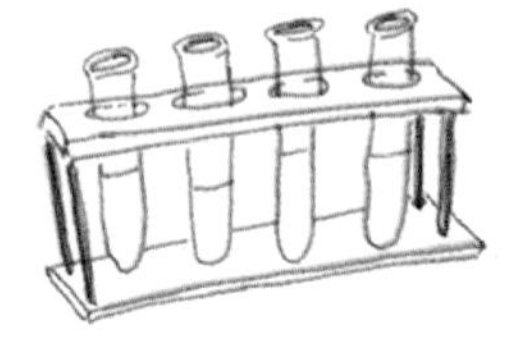

Then Mark pressed the purple button
and the blue-eyed creature vanished.

Flying home on the winged monster, he used the Molecule Maker to repair the trees, cars and fire hydrant. That's when he noticed police cars and fire engines racing along with sirens blaring and lights flashing. People were gathering in the streets, and Mark could see others staring through windows. Luckily, he was high in the air and nobody thought to look up there.

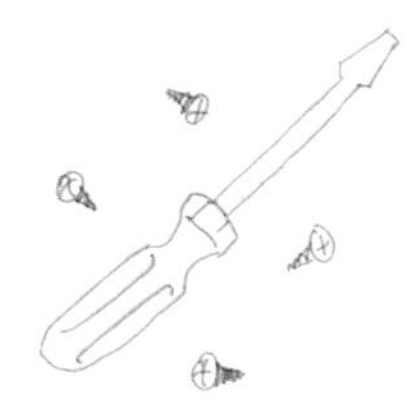

After a smooth landing in the front yard, Mark disintegrated the flying dinosaur. Then, from inside the laboratory, he fixed the broken window. Thinking he had escaped punishment, Mark breathed a sigh of relief. But as he turned to replace the Molecule Maker, what he saw sent chills down his spine.

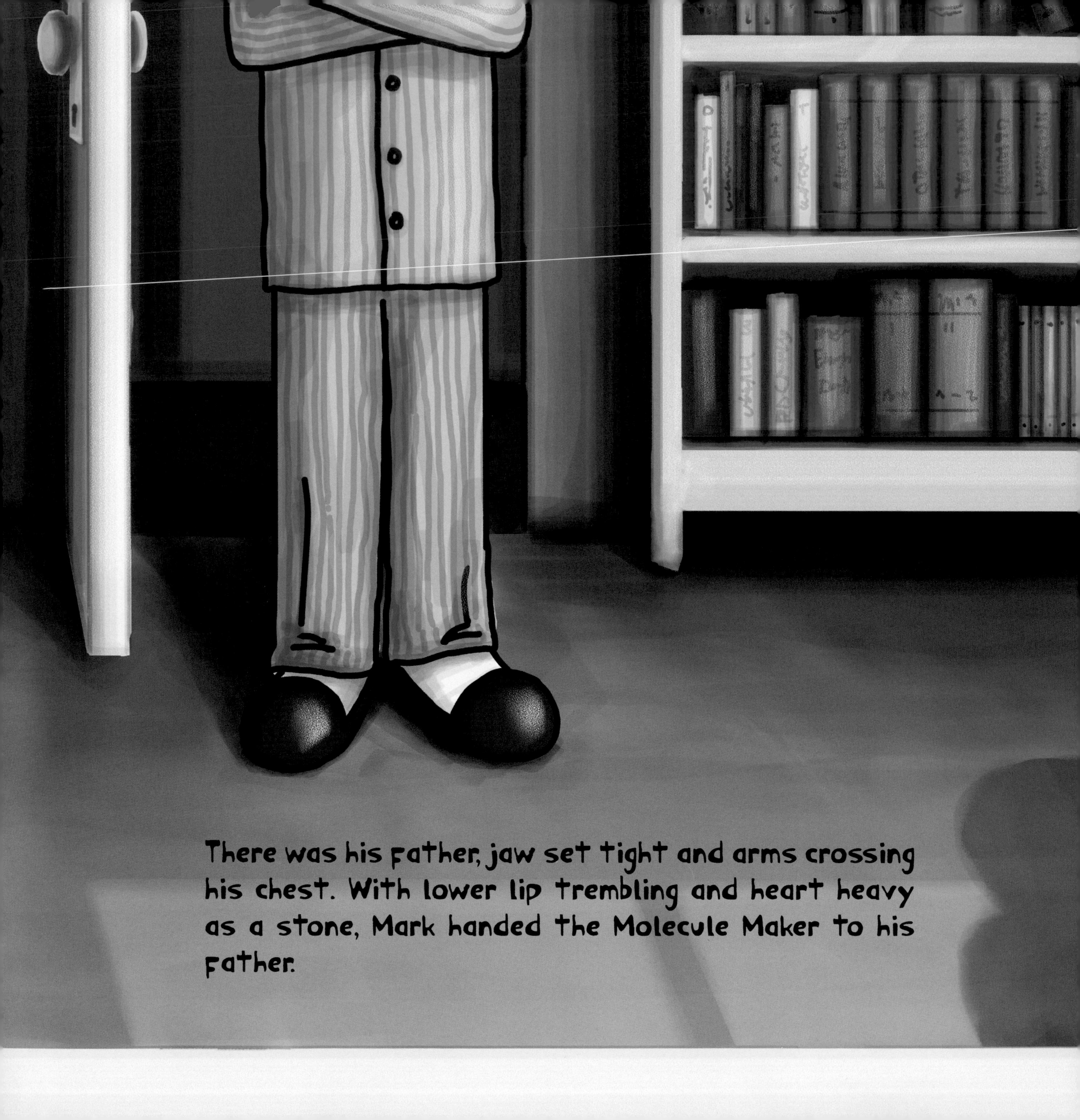

There was his father, jaw set tight and arms crossing his chest. With lower lip trembling and heart heavy as a stone, Mark handed the Molecule Maker to his father.

"The rules are for your safety, Son," his father said. "I love you very much and could never forgive myself if anything happened to you."

"I'm sorry, Dad. I'll never come in here again, I promise. Not without you."

Outside, the sun was rising.

As Mark turned to leave the laboratory, his father placed a hand on his shoulder, and said with a wink, "Wait a minute, Son. Let me show you what this Molecule Maker can really do."

Mark smiled as his father grabbed his lab coat and slipped his arms through the sleeves. It was a new day, and Mark followed his father, his eyes as wide as the sky.

Also from
OCTOPUS INK PRESS

Silly the Seed

Silly the Seed is the heroic adventure of a small seed that grows up to be a beautiful flower. Along the way his acts of friendship and kindness teach and entertain readers of all ages. But when Silly needs help, who will help him?

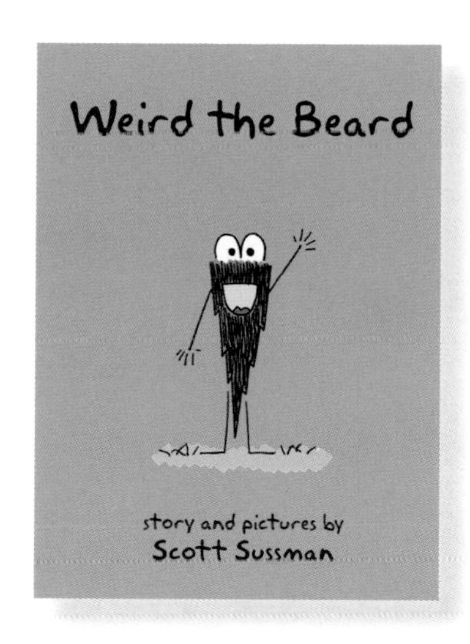

Weird the Beard

Weird the Beard is the amusing journey of a beard that makes friends by cracking jokes. But the joke's on Weird when he tries to befriend a suspicious-looking razor. Needless to say, he will never be the same.

COMING SOON!

Fred and the Monster

Fred is afraid of the dark. So is the monster under his bed. One night, Fred's mom does the unthinkable... she turns off the light! Stricken with terror, Fred and the monster must rely on each other for the courage to confront their worst fear.